Helena Petrov

A Bewitched Life

INTRODUCTION

It was a dark, chilly night in September, 1884. A heavy gloom had descended over the streets of A---, a small town on the Rhine, and was hanging like a black funeral-pall over the dull factory burgh. The greater number of its inhabitants, wearied by their long day's work, had hours before retired to stretch their tired limbs, and lay their aching heads upon their pillows. All was quiet in the large house; all was quiet in the deserted streets.
I too was lying in my bed; alas, not one of rest, but of pain and sickness, to which I had been confined for some days. So still was everything in the house, that, as Longfellow has it, its stillness seemed almost audible. I could plainly hear the murmur of the blood as it rushed through my aching body, producing that monotonous singing so familiar to one who lends a watchful ear to silence. I had listened to it until, in my nervous imagination, it had grown into the sound of a distant cataract, the fall of mighty waters... when, suddenly changing its character, the evergrowing "singing" merged into other and far more welcome sounds. It was the low, and at first scarce audible, whisper of a human voice. It approached, and gradually strengthening seemed to speak in my very ear. Thus sounds a voice speaking across a blue quiescent lake, in one of those wondrously acoustic gorges of the snow-capped mountains, where the air is so pure that a word pronounced half a mile off seems almost at the elbow. Yes; it was the voice of

one whom to know is to reverence; of one, to me, owing to many mystic associations, most dear and holy; a voice familiar for long years and ever welcome; doubly so in hours of mental or physical suffering, for it always brings with it a ray of hope and consolation.

"Courage," it whispered in gentle, mellow tones. "Think of the days passed by you in sweet associations; of the great lessons received of Nature's truths; of the many errors of men concerning these truths; and try to add to them the experience of a night in this city. Let the narrative of a strange life, that will interest you, help to shorten the hours of suffering.....Give your attention. Look yonder before you!"

"Yonder" meant the clear, large windows of an empty house on the other side of the narrow street of the German town. They faced my own in almost a straight line across the street, and my bed faced the windows of my sleeping room. Obedient to the suggestion, I directed my gaze towards them, and what I saw made me for the time being forget the agony of the pain that racked my swollen arm and rheumatical body.

Over the windows was creeping a mist; a dense, heavy, serpentine, whitish mist, that looked like the huge shadow of a gigantic boa slowly uncoiling its body. Gradually it disappeared, to leave a lustrous light, soft and silvery, as though the window-panes behind reflected a thousand moonbeams, a tropical star-lit sky--first from outside, then from within the empty rooms. Next I saw the mist elongating itself and throwing, as it were, a fairy bridge across the street from the bewitched windows to my own balcony, nay, to my very own bed. As I continued gazing, the wall and windows and the opposite house itself, suddenly vanished. The space occupied by the empty rooms had changed into the interior of another smaller room, in what I knew to be a

Swiss chalet--into a study, whose old, dark walls were covered from floor to ceiling with book shelves on which were many antiquated folios, as well as works of a more recent date. In the centre stood a large old-fashioned table, littered over with manuscripts and writing materials. Before it, quill-pen in hand, sat an old man; a grim-looking, skeleton-like personage, with a face so thin, so pale, yellow and emaciated, that the light of the solitary little student's lamp was reflected in two shining spots on his high cheekbones, as though they were carved out of ivory.

As I tried to get a better view of him by slowly raising myself upon my pillows, the whole vision, chalet and study, desk, books and scribe, seemed to flicker and move. Once set in motion, they approached nearer and nearer, until, gliding noiselessly along the fleecy bridge of clouds across the street, they floated through the closed windows into my room and finally seemed to settle beside my bed.

"Listen to what he thinks and is going to write"--said in soothing tones the same familiar, far off, and yet near voice. "Thus you will hear a narrative, the telling of which may help to shorten the long sleepless hours, and even make you forget for a while your pain...Try!"--it added, using the well-known Rosicrucian and Kabalistic formula.

I tried, doing as I was bid. I centred all my attention on the solitary laborious figure that I saw before me, but which did not see me. At first, the noise of the quill-pen with which the old man was writing, suggested to my mind nothing more than a low whispered murmur of a nondescript nature. Then, gradually, my ear caught the indistinct words of a faint and distant voice, and I thought the figure before me, bending over its manuscript, was reading its tale aloud instead of writing it. But I soon found out my error. For casting my gaze at the old scribe's face, I saw at a glance that his lips were compressed and motionless, and the voice too thin and shrill to be his voice. Stranger still at every word traced by the feeble, aged hand, I noticed a light flashing from under his pen, a bright coloured spark that became instantaneously a sound, or--what is the same thing--it seemed to do so to my inner perceptions. It was indeed the small voice of the quill that I heard though scribe and pen were at the time, perchance, hundreds of miles away from Germany. Such things will happen occasionally, especially at night, beneath whose starry shade, as Byron tells us.

"...we learn the language of another world..."

However it may be, the words uttered by the quill remained in my memory for days after. Nor had I any great difficulty in retaining them, for when I sat down to record the story, I found it, as usual, indelibly impressed on the astral tablets before my inner eye.

Thus, I had but to copy it and so give it as I received it. I failed to learn the name of the unknown nocturnal writer. Nevertheless, though the reader may prefer to regard the whole story as one made up for the occasion, a dream, perhaps, still its incidents will, I hope, prove none the less interesting.

I--THE STRANGER'S STORY

My birth-place is a small mountain hamlet, a cluster of Swiss cottages, hidden deep in a sunny nook, between two tumble-down glaciers and a peak covered with eternal snows. Thither, thirty-seven years ago, I returned--crippled mentally and physically--to die, if death would only have me. The pure, invigorating air of my birth-place decided otherwise. I am still alive; perhaps for the purpose of giving evidence to facts I have kept profoundly secret from all--a tale of horror I would rather hide than reveal. The reason for this unwillingness on my part is due to my early education, and to subsequent events that gave the lie to my most cherished prejudices. Some people might be inclined to regard these events as providential: I, however, believe in no Providence, and yet am unable to attribute them to mere chance. I connect them as the ceaseless evolution of effects, engendered by certain direct causes, with one primary and fundamental cause, from which ensued all that followed. A feeble old man am I now, yet physical weakness has in no way impared my mental faculties. I remember the smallest details of that terrible cause, which engendered such fatal results. It is these which furnish me with an additional proof of the actual existence of one whom I fain would regard--oh, that I could do so!--as a creature born of my fancy, the evanescent production of a feverish, horrid dream! Oh that terrible, mild and all-forgiving, that saintly and respected Being! It was that paragon of all the virtues who embittered my whole existence. It is he, who, pushing me violently out of the monotonous but secure groove of daily life, was the first to force upon me the certitude of a life hereafter, thus adding an additional horror to one already great enough.

With a view to a clearer comprehension of the situation, I must interrupt these recollections with a few words about myself. Oh how, if I could, would I obliterate that hated Self!

Born in Switzerland, of French parents, who centred the whole world-wisdom in the literary trinity of Voltaire, J. J. Rousseau and D'Holbach, and educated in a German university, I grew up a thorough materialist, a confirmed atheist. I could never have even pictured to myself any beings--least of all a Being--above or even outside visible nature, as distinguished from her. Hence I regarded everything that could not be brought under the strictest analysis of the physical senses as a mere chimera. A soul, I argued, even supposing man has one, must be material. According to Origen's definition, incorporeus--the epithet he gave to his God--signifies a substance only more subtle than that of physical bodies, of which, at best, we can form no definite idea. How then can that, of which our senses cannot enable us to obtain any clear knowledge, how can that make itself visible or produce any tangible manifestations?

Accordingly, I received the tales of nascent Spiritualism with a feeling of utter contempt, and regarded the overtures made by certain priests with derision, often akin to anger. And indeed the latter feeling has never entirely abandoned me.

Pascal, in the eighth Act of his "Thoughts," confesses to a most complete incertitude upon the existence of God. Throughout my life, I too professed a complete certitude as to the non-existence of any such extra-cosmic being, and repeated with that great thinker the memorable words in which he tells us: "I have examined if this God of whom all the world speaks might not have left some marks of himself. I look everywhere, and everywhere I see nothing but obscurity. Nature offers me nothing that may not be a matter of doubt and inquietude." Nor have I found to this day anything that might unsettle me in precisely similar and even stronger feelings. I have never believed, nor shall I ever believe, in a Supreme Being. But at the potentialities of man, proclaimed far and wide in the East, powers so developed in some persons as to make them virtually Gods, at them I laugh no more. My whole broken life is a protest against such negation. I believe in such phenomena, and--I curse them, whenever they come, and by whatsoever means generated.

On the death of my parents, owing to an unfortunate lawsuit, I lost the greater part of my fortune, and resolved--for the sake of those I loved best, rather than for my own--to make another for myself. My elder sister, whom I adored, had married a poor man. I accepted the offer of a rich Hamburg firm and sailed for Japan as its junior partner.

For several years my business went on successfully. I got into the confidence of many influential Japanese, through whose protection I was enabled to travel and transact business in many localities, which, in those days especially, were not easily accessible to foreigners. Indifferent to every religion, I became interested in the philosophy of Buddhism, the only religious system I thought worthy of being called philosophical. Thus, in my moments of leisure, I visited the most remarkable temples of Japan, the most important and curious of the ninety-six Buddhist monasteries of Kioto. I have examined in turn Day--Bootzoo, with its gigantic bell; Tzeonene, Enarino-Yassero, Kie-Missoo, Higadzi-Hong-Vonsi, and many other famous temples.

Several years passed away, and during that whole period I was not cured of my scepticism, nor did I ever contemplate having my opinions on this subject altered. I derided the pretensions of the Japanese bonzes and ascetics, as I had those of Christian priests and European Spiritualists. I could not believe in the acquisition of powers unknown to, and never studied by, men of science; hence I scoffed at all such ideas. The superstitious and atrabilious Buddhist, teaching us to shun the pleasures of life, to put to rout one's passions, to render oneself insensible alike to happiness and suffering, in order to acquire such chimerical powers--seemed supremely ridiculous in my eyes.

On a day ever memorable to me--a fatal day--I made the acquaintance of a venerable and learned Bonze, a Japanese priest, named Tamoora Hideyeri. I met him at the foot of the golden Kwon-On, and from that moment he became my best and most trusted friend. Notwithstanding my great and genuine regard for him, however, whenever a good opportunity was offered I never failed to mock his religious convictions, thereby very often hurting his feelings.

But my old friend was as meek and forgiving as any true Buddhist's heart might desire. He never resented my impatient sarcasms, even when they were, to say the least, of equivocal propriety, and generally limited his replies to the "wait and see" kind of protest. Nor could he be brought to seriously believe in the sincerity of my denial of the existence of any God or Gods. The full meaning of the terms "atheism" and "scepticism" was beyond the comprehension of his otherwise extremely intellectual and acute mind. Like certain reverential Christians, he seemed incapable of realizing that any man of sense should prefer the wise conclusions arrived at by philosophy and modern science to a ridiculous belief in an invisible world full of Gods and spirits, dzins and demons. "Man is a spiritual being," he insisted, "who returns to earth more than once, and is rewarded or punished in the between times." The proposition that man is nothing else but a heap of organized dust, was beyond him. Like Jeremy Collier, he refused to admit that he was no better than "a stalking machine, a speaking head without a soul in it," whose "thoughts" are all bound by the laws of motion. "For," he argued, "if my actions were, as you say, prescribed beforehand, and I had no more liberty or free will to change the course of my action than the running waters of the river yonder, then the glorious doctrine of Karma, of merit and demerit, would be a foolishness indeed."

Thus the whole of my hyper-metaphysical friend's ontology rested on the shaky superstructure of metempsychosis, of a fancied "just" Law of Retribution, and other such equally absurd dreams.

"We cannot," said he paradoxically one day, "hope to live hereafter in the full enjoyment of our consciousness, unless we have built for it beforehand a firm and solid foundation of spirituality.....Nay, laugh not, friend of no faith," he meekly pleaded, "but rather think and reflect on this. One who has never taught himself to live in Spirit during his conscious and responsible life on earth, can hardly hope to enjoy a sentient existence after death, when, deprived of his body, he is limited to that Spirit alone."

"What can you mean by life in Spirit?"--I enquired.

"Life on a spiritual plane; that which the Buddhists call Tushita Devaloka (Paradise). Man can create such a blissful existence for himself between two births, by the gradual transference on to that plane of all the faculties which during his sojourn on earth manifest through his organic body and, as you call it, animal brain."

"How absurd! And how can man do this?"

"Contemplation and a strong desire to assimilate the blessed Gods, will enable him to do so."

"And if man refuses this intellectual occupation, by which you mean, I suppose, the fixing of the eyes on the tip of his nose, what becomes of him after the death of his body?" was my mocking question.

"He will be dealt with according to the prevailing state of his consciousness, of which there are many grades. At best--immediate rebirth; at worst--the state of avitchi, a mental hell. Yet one need not be an ascetic to assimilate spiritual life which will extend to the hereafter. All that is required is to try and approach Spirit."

"How so? Even when disbelieving in it?"--I rejoined.

"Even so! One may disbelieve and yet harbour in one's nature room for doubt, however small that room may be, and thus try one day, were it but for one moment, to open the door of the inner temple; and this will prove sufficient for the purpose."

"You are decidedly poetical, and paradoxical to boot, reverend sir. Will you kindly explain to me a little more of the mystery?"

"There is none; still I am willing. Suppose for a moment that some unknown temple to which you have never been before, and the existence of which you think you have reasons to deny, is the 'spiritual plane' of which I am speaking. Some one takes you by the hand and leads you towards its entrance, curiosity makes you open its door and look within. By this simple act, by entering it for one second, you have established an everlasting connection between your consciousness and the temple. You cannot deny its existence any longer, nor obliterate the fact of your having entered it. And according to the character and the variety of your work, within its holy precincts, so will you live in it af-

ter your consciousness is severed from its dwelling of flesh."
"What do you mean? And what has my after-death consciousness--if such a thing exists--to do with the temple?"
"It has everything to do with it," solemnly rejoined the old man. "There can be no self-consciousness after death outside the temple of spirit. That which you will have done within its plane will alone survive. All the rest is false and an illusion. It is doomed to perish in the Ocean of Maya."
Amused at the idea of living outside one's body, I urged on my old friend to tell me more. Mistaking my meaning the venerable man willingly consented.
Tamoora Hideyeri belonged to the great temple of Tzionene, a Buddhist monastery, famous not only in all Japan, but also throughout Tibet and China. No other is so venerated in Kioto. Its monks belong to the sect of Dzeno-doo, and are considered as the most learned among the many erudite fraternities. They are, moreover, closely connected and allied with the Yamabooshi (the ascetics, or hermits), who follow the doctrines of Lao-tze. No wonder, that at the slightest provocation on my part the priest flew into the highest metaphysics, hoping thereby to cure me of my infidelity.
No use repeating here the long rigmarole of the most hopelessly involved and incomprehensible of all doctrines. According to his ideas, we have to train ourselves for spirituality in another world--as for gymnastics. Carrying on the analogy between the temple and the "spiritual plane" he tried to illustrate his idea. He had himself worked in the temple of Spirit two-thirds of his life, and given several hours daily to "contemplation." Thus he knew that after he had laid aside his mortal casket, "a mere illusion," he explained--he would in his spiritual consciousness live over again every feeling of ennobling joy and divine bliss he had

ever had, or ought to have had--only a hundredfold intensified. His work on the spirit-plane had been considerable, he said, and he hoped, therefore that the wages of the labourer would prove proportionate.

"But suppose the labourer, as in the example you have just brought forward in my case, should have no more, than opened the temple door out of mere curiosity; had only peeped into the sanctuary never to set his foot therein again. What then?"

"Then," he answered, "you would have only this short minute to record in your future self-consciousness and no more. Our life hereafter records and repeats but the impressions and feelings we have had in our spiritual experiences and nothing else. Thus, if instead of reverence at the moment of entering the abode of Spirit, you had been harbouring in your heart anger, jealousy or grief, then your future spiritual life would be a sad one, in truth. There would be nothing to record, save the opening of a door, in a fit of bad temper."

"How then could it be repeated?"--I insisted, highly amused. "What do you suppose I would be doing before incarnating again?"

"In that case," he said speaking slowly and weighing every word--"in that case, you would have I fear, only to open and shut the temple door, over and over again, during a period which, however short, would seem to you an eternity."

This kind of after-death occupation appeared to me, at that time, so grotesque in its sublime absurdity, that I was seized with an almost inextinguishable fit of laughter.

My venerable friend looked considerably dismayed at such a result of his metaphysical instruction. He had evidently not expected such hilarity. However, he said nothing, but only sighed and gazed at me with increased benevolence and pity shining in his small black eyes.

"Pray excuse my laughter," I apologized. "But really, now, you cannot seriously mean to tell me that the 'spiritual state' you advocate and so firmly believe in, consists only in aping certain things we do in life?"

"Nay, nay; not aping, but only intensifying their repetition; filling the gaps that were unjustly left unfilled during life in the fruition of our acts and deeds, and of everything performed on the spiritual plane of the one real state. What I said was an illustration, and no doubt for you, who seem entirely ignorant of the mysteries of Soul-Vision, not a very intelligible one. It is myself who am to be blamed.....What I sought to impress upon you was that, as the spiritual state of our consciousness liberated from its body is but the fruition of every spiritual act performed during life, where an act had been barren, there could be no results expected--save the repetition of that act itself. This is all. I pray you may be spared such fruitless deeds and finally made to see certain truths." And passing through the usual Japanese courtesies of taking leave the excellent man departed.

Alas, alas! had I but known at the time what I have learnt since, how little would I have laughed, and how much more would I have learned!

But as the matter stood, the more personal affection and respect I felt for him, the less could I become reconciled to his wild ideas about an after-life, and especially as to the acquisition by some men of supernatural powers. I felt particularly disgusted with his reverence for the Yamabooshi, the allies of every Buddhist sect in the land. Their claims to the "miraculous" were simply odious to my notions. To hear every Jap I knew at Kioto, even to my own partner, the shrewdest of all the business men I had come across in the East--mentioning these followers of Lao-tze with downcast eyes, reverentially folded hands, and affirmations of their possessing "great" and "wonderful" gifts, was more than I was prepared to patiently tolerate in those days. And who were they, after all, these great magicians with their ridiculous pretensions to super-mundane knowledge; these "holy beggars" who, as I then thought, purposely dwell in the recesses of unfrequented mountains and an unapproachable craggy steeps, so as the better to afford no chance to curious intruders of finding them out and watching them in their own dens? Simply, impudent fortune-tellers, Japanese gypsies who sell charms and talismans, and no better. In answer to those who sought to assure me that though the Yamabooshi lead a mysterious life, admitting none of the profane to their secrets, they still do accept pupils, however difficult it is for one to become their disciple, and that thus they have living witnesses to the great purity and sanctity of their lives, in answer to such affirmations I opposed the strongest negation and stood firmly by it. I insulted both masters and pupils, classing them under the same category of fools, when not knaves, and I went so far as to include in this number the Sintos. Now Sintoism or Sin-Syu, "faith in the Gods, and in the way to the Gods," that is, belief in the communication between these creatures and men, is a kind of worship of nature-spirits, than which nothing can be more miserably absurd. And by placing the Sintos among the fools and knaves of other sects, I gained many enemies. For the Sinto Kanusi (spiritual teachers) are looked upon as the highest in the upper classes of Society, the Mikado himself being at the head of their hierarchy and the members of the sect belonging to the most cultured and educated men in Japan. These Kanusi of the Sinto form no caste or class apart, nor do they pass any ordination--at any rate none known to outsiders. And as they claim publicly no special privilege or powers, even their dress being in no wise different from that of the laity, but are simply in the world's opinion professors and students of occult and spiritual sciences, I very often came in contact with them without in the least suspecting that I was in the presence of such personages.

II--THE MYSTERIOUS VISITOR

Years passed; and as time went by, my ineradicable scepticism grew stronger and waxed fiercer every day. I have already mentioned an elder and much-beloved sister, my only surviving relative. She had married and had lately gone to live at Nuremberg. I regarded her with feelings more filial than fraternal, and her children were as dear to me as might have been my own. At the time of the great catastrophe that in the course of a few days had made my father lose his large fortune, and my mother break her heart, she it was, that sweet big sister of mine, who had made herself of her own accord the guardian angel of our ruined family. Out of her great love for me, her younger brother, for whom she attempted to replace the professors that could no longer be afforded, she had renounced her own happiness. She sacrificed herself and the man she loved, by indefinitely postponing their marriage, in order to help our father and chiefly myself by her undivided devotion. And, oh, how I loved and reverenced her, time but strengthening this earliest family affection! They who maintain that no atheist, as such, can be a true friend, an affectionate relative, or a loyal subject, utter--whether consciously or unconsciously--the greatest calumny and lie. To say that a materialist grows hard-hearted as he grows older, that he cannot love as a believer does, is simply the greatest fallacy.

There may be such exceptional cases, it is true, but these are found only occasionally in men who are even more selfish

than they are sceptical, or vulgarly worldly. But when a man who is kindly disposed in his nature, for no selfish motives but because of reason and love of truth, becomes what is called atheistical, he is only strengthened in his family affections, and in his sympathies with his fellow men. All his emotions, all the ardent aspirations towards the unseen and unreachable, all the love which he would otherwise have uselessly bestowed on a supposititional heaven and its God, become now centred with tenfold force upon his loved ones and mankind. Indeed, the atheist's heart alone---
...can know.
What secret tides of still enjoyment flow When brothers love...
It was such holy fraternal love that led me also to sacrifice my comfort and personal welfare to secure her happiness, the felicity of her who had been more than a mother to me. I was a mere youth when I left home for Hamburg. There, working with all the desperate earnestness of a man who has but one noble object in view--to relieve suffering, and help those whom he loves--I very soon secured the confidence of my employers, who raised me in consequence to the high post of trust I always enjoyed. My first real pleasure and reward in life was to see my sister married to the man she had sacrificed for my sake, and to help them in their struggle for existence.

So purifying and unselfish was this affection of mine for her that, when it came to be shared among her children, instead of losing in intensity by such division, it seemed to only grow the stronger. Born with the potentiality of the warmest family affection in me, the devotion for my sister was so great, that the thought of burning that sacred fire of love before any idol, save that of herself and family, never entered my head. This was the only, church I recognized, the only church wherein I worshipped at the altar of holy family affection. In fact this large family of eleven persons, including her husband, was the only tie that attached me to Europe. Twice, during a period of nine years, had I crossed the ocean with the sole object of seeing and pressing these dear ones to my heart. I had no other business in the West; and having performed this pleasant duty, I returned each time to Japan to work and toil for them. For their sake I remained a bachelor, that the wealth I might acquire should go undivided to them alone.

We had always corresponded as regularly as the long transit of the then very irregular service of the mail-boats would permit. But suddenly there came a break in my letters from home. For nearly a year I received no intelligence; and day by day, I became more restless, more apprehensive of some great misfortune. Vainly I looked for a letter, a simple message; and my efforts to account for so unusual a silence were fruitless.

"Friend," said to me one day Tamoora Hideyeri, my only confidant, "Friend, consult a holy Yamabooshi--and you will feel at rest."

Of course the offer was rejected with as much moderation as I could command under the provocation. But, as steamer after steamer came in without a word of news, I felt a despair which daily increased in depth and fixity. This finally degenerated into an irrepressible craving, a morbid desire to learn--the worst, as I then thought. I struggled hard with the feeling, but it had the best of me. Only a few months before a complete master of myself--I now became an abject slave to fear. A fatalist of the school of D'Holbach, I, who had always regarded belief in the system of necessity as being the only promoter of philosophical happiness, and as having the most advantageous influence over human weaknesses, I felt a craving for something akin to fortune-telling! I had gone so far as to forget the first principle of my doctrine--the only one calculated to calm our sorrows, to inspire us with a useful submission, namely a rational resignation to the decrees of blind destiny, with which foolish sensibility causes us so often to be overwhelmed--the doctrine that all is necessary. Yes; forgetting this, I was drawn into a shameful, superstitious longing, a stupid, disgraceful desire to learn--if not futurity, at any rate that which was taking place at the other side of the globe. My conduct seemed utterly modified, my temperament and aspirations wholly changed; and like a weak, nervous girl, I caught myself straining my mind to the very verge of lunacy in an attempt to look--as I had been told one could sometimes do--beyond the oceans, and learn, at last, the real cause of this long, inexplicable silence!

One evening, at sunset, my old friend, the venerable Bonze, Tamoora, appeared on the verandah of my low wooden house. I had not visited him for many days, and he had come to know how I was. I took the opportunity to once more sneer at one, whom, in reality, I regarded with most affectionate respect. With equivocal taste for which I repented almost before the words had been pronounced--I enquired of him why he had taken the trouble to walk all that distance when he might have learned anything he liked about me by simply interrogating a Yamabooshi? He seemed a little hurt, at first; but after keenly scrutinizing my dejected face, he mildly remarked that he could only insist upon what he had advised before. Only one of that holy order could give me consolation in my present state.

From that instant, an insane desire possessed me to challenge him to prove his assertions. I defied--I said to him--any and every one of his alleged magicians to tell me the name of the person I was thinking of, and what he was doing at that moment. He quietly answered that my desire could be easily satisfied. There was a Yamabooshi two doors from me, visiting a sick Sinto. He would fetch him--if I only said the word.

I said it and from the moment of its utterance my doom was sealed.

How shall I find words to describe the scene that followed! Twenty minutes after the desire had been so incautiously expressed, an old Japanese, uncommonly tall and majestic for one of that race, pale, thin and emaciated, was standing before me. There, where I had expected to find servile obsequiousness, I only discerned an air of calm and dignified composure, the attitude of one who knows his moral superiority, and therefore scorns to notice the mistakes of those who fail to recognize it. To the somewhat irreverent and mocking questions, which I put to him one after another, with feverish eagerness, he made no reply; but gazed on me in silence as a physician would look at a delirious patient. From the moment he fixed--his eyes on mine, I felt--or shall I say, saw--as though it were a sharp ray of light, a thin silvery thread, shoot out from the intensely black and narrow eyes so deeply sunk in the yellow old face. It seemed to penetrate into my brain and heart like an arrow, and set to work to dig out, there from every thought and feeling. Yes; I both saw and felt it, and very soon the double sensation became intolerable.

To break the spell I defied him to tell me what he had found in my thoughts. Calmly came the correct answer--Extreme anxiety for a female relative, her husband and children, who were inhabiting a house the correct description of which he gave as though he knew it as well as myself. I turned a suspicious eye upon my friend, the Bonze, to whose indiscretions, I thought, I was indebted for the quick reply. Remembering however that Tamoora could know nothing of the appearance of my sister's house, that the Japanese are proverbially truthful and, as friends, faithful to death--I felt ashamed of my suspicion. To atone for it before my own conscience I asked the hermit whether he could tell me anything of the present state of that beloved sister of mine. The foreigner--was the reply--would never believe in the words, or trust to the knowledge of any person but himself. Were the Yamabooshi to tell him, the impression would wear out hardly a few hours later, and the inquirer find himself as miserable as before. There was but one means; and that was to make the foreigner (myself) see with his own eyes, and thus learn the truth for himself. Was the enquirer ready to be placed by a Yamabooshi, a stranger to him, in the required state?

I had heard in Europe of mesmerized somnambules and pretenders to clairvoyance, and having no faith in them, I had, therefore, nothing against the process itself. Even in the midst of my never-ceasing mental agony, I could not help smiling at the ridiculous nature of the operation I was willingly submitting to. Nevertheless I silently bowed consent.

III--PSYCHIC MAGIC

The old Yamabooshi lost no time. He looked at the setting sun, and finding, probably, the Lord Ten-Dzio-Dai-Dzio (the Spirit who darts his Rays) propitious for the coming ceremony, he speedily drew out a little bundle. It contained a small lacquered box, a piece of vegetable paper, made from the bark of the mulberry tree, and a pen, with which he traced upon the paper a few sentences in the Naiden character--a peculiar style of written language used only for religious and mystical purposes. Having finished, he exhibited from under his clothes a small round mirror of steel of extraordinary brilliancy, and placing it before my eyes asked me to look into it.

I had not only heard before of these mirrors, which are frequently used in the temples, but I had often seen them. It is claimed that under the direction and will of instructed priests, there appear in them the Daij-Dzin, the great spirits who notify the enquiring devotees of their fate. I first imagined that his intention was to evoke such a spirit, who would answer my queries. What happened, however, was something of quite a different character.

No sooner had I, not without a last pang of mental squeamishness, produced by a deep sense of my own absurd position, touched the mirror, than I suddenly felt a strange sensation in the arm of the hand that held it. For a brief moment I forgot to "sit in the seat of the scorner" and failed to look at the matter from a ludicrous point of view. Was it

fear that suddenly clutched my brain, for an instant paralyzing its activity---
...that fear when the heart longs to know.
what it is death to hear?
No; for I still had consciousness enough left to go on persuading myself that nothing would come out of an experiment, in the nature of which no sane man could ever believe. What was it then, that crept across my brain like a living thing of ice, producing therein a sensation of horror, and then clutched at my heart as if a deadly serpent had fastened its fangs into it? With a convulsive jerk of the hand I dropped the--I blush to write the adjective--"magic" mirror, and could not force myself to pick it up from the settee on which I was reclining. For one short moment there was a terrible struggle between some undefined, and to me utterly inexplicable, longing to look into the depths of the polished surface of the mirror and my pride, the ferocity of which nothing seemed capable of taming. It was finally so tamed, however, its revolt being conquered by its own defiant intensity. There was an opened novel lying on a lacquer table near the settee, and as my eyes happened to fall upon its pages, I read the words, "The veil which covers futurity is woven by the hand of mercy." This was enough. That same pride which had hitherto held me back from what I regarded as a degrading, superstitious experiment, caused me to challenge my fate. I picked up the ominously shining disk and prepared to look into it.

While I was examining the mirror, the Yamabooshi hastily spoke a few words to the Bonze, Tamoora, at which I threw a furtive and suspicious glance at both. I was wrong once more.

"The holy man desires me to put you a question and give you at the same time a warning," remarked the Bonze. "If you are willing to see for yourself now, you will have--under the penalty of seeing for ever, in the hereafter, all that is taking place, at whatever distance, and that against your will or inclination--to submit to a regular course of purification, after you have learnt what you want through the mirror."

"What is this course, and what have I to promise?" I asked defiantly.

"It is for your own good. You must promise him to submit to the process, lest, for the rest of his life, he should have to hold himself responsible, before his own conscience, for having made an irresponsible seer of you. Will you do so, friend?"

"There will be time enough to think of it, if I see anything"--I sneeringly replied, adding under my breath--"something I doubt a good deal, so far."

"Well you are warned, friend. The consequences will now remain with yourself," was the solemn answer.

I glanced at the clock, and made a gesture of impatience, which was remarked and understood by the Yamabooshi. It was just seven minutes after five.

"Define well in your mind what you would see and learn," said the "conjuror," placing the mirror and paper in my hands, and instructing me how to use them.

His instructions were received by me with more impatience than gratitude; and for one short instant, I hesitated again. Nevertheless, I replied, while fixing the mirror.

"I desire but one thing--to learn the reason or reasons why my sister has so suddenly ceased writing to me.". . .

Had I pronounced these words in reality, and in the hearing of the two witnesses, or had I only thought them? To this day I cannot decide the point. I now remember but one thing distinctly: while I sat gazing in the mirror, the Yamabooshi kept gazing at me. But whether this process lasted half a second or three hours, I have never since been able to settle in my mind with any degree of satisfaction. I can recall every detail of the scene up to that moment when I took up the mirror with the left hand, holding the paper inscribed with the mystic characters between the thumb and finger of the right, when all of a sudden I seemed to quite lose consciousness of the surrounding objects. The passage from the active waking state to one that I could compare with nothing I had ever experienced before, was so rapid, that while my eyes had ceased to perceive external objects and had completely lost sight of the Bonze, the Yamabooshi, and even of my room, I could nevertheless distinctly see the whole of my head and my back, as I sat leaning forward with the mirror in my hand. Then came a strong sensation or an involuntary rush forward, of snapping off, so to say, from my place--I had almost said from my body. And, then, while every one of my other senses had become totally paralyzed, my eyes, as I thought, unexpectedly caught a clearer and far more vivid glimpse than they had ever had in reality, of my sister's new house at Nuremberg, which I had never visited and knew only from a sketch, and other scenery with which I had never been very familiar. Together with this, and while feeling in my brain what seemed like flashes of a departing consciousness--dying persons must feel so, no doubt--the very last, vague thought, so weak as to have been hardly perceptible, was that I must look very, very ridiculous...This feeling--for such it was rather than a thought--was interrupted, suddenly extinguished, so to say, by a clear mental vision (I cannot characterize it otherwise) of myself, of that which I regarded as, and knew to be my body, lying with ashy cheeks on a settee, dead to all intents and purposes, but still staring with the cold and glassy eyes of a corpse into the mirror. Bending over it, with his two emaciated hands cutting the air in every direction over its white face, stood the tall figure of the Yamabooshi, for whom I felt at that instant an inextinguishable, murderous hatred. As I was going, in thought, to pounce upon the vile charlatan, my corpse, the two old men, the room itself, and every object in it, trembled and danced in a reddish glowing light, and seemed to float rapidly away from "me." A few more grotesque, distorted shadows before "my" sight; and, with a last feeling of terror and a supreme effort to realize who then was I now, since I was not that corpse--a great veil of darkness fell over me, like a funeral pall, and every thought in me was dead.

IV--A VISION OF HORROR

How strange! ... Where was I now? It was evident to me that I had once more returned to my senses. For there I was, vividly realizing that I was rapidly moving forward, while experiencing a queer, strange sensation as though I were swimming, without impulse or effort on my part, and in total darkness. The idea that first presented itself to me was that of a long subterranean passage of water, of earth, and stifling air, though bodily I had no perception, no sensation, of the presence or contact of any of these. I tried to utter a few words, to repeat my last sentence, "I desire but one thing: to learn the reason or reasons why my sister has so suddenly ceased writing to me"--but the only words I heard out of the twenty-one, were the two, "to learn," and these, instead of their coming out of my own larynx, came back to me in my own voice, but entirely outside myself, near, but not in me. In short, they were pronounced by my voice, not by my lips...

One more rapid, involuntary motion, one more plunge into the Cymmerian darkness of a (to me) unknown element, and I saw myself standing--actually standing underground, as it seemed. I was compactly and thickly surrounded on all sides, above and below, right and left, with earth, and in the mould, and yet it weighed not, and seemed quite immaterial and transparent to my senses. I did not realize for one second the utter absurdity, nay, impossibility of that seeming fact! One second more, one short instant, and I perceived--oh, inexpressible horror, when I think of it now; for then, although I perceived, realized, and recorded facts and events far more clearly than ever I had done before, I did not seem to be touched in any other way by what I saw. Yes--I perceived a coffin at my feet. It was a plain, unpretentious shell, made of deal, the last couch of the pauper, in which, notwithstanding its closed lid, I plainly saw a hideous, grinning skull, a man's skeleton, mutilated and broken in many of its parts, as though it had been taken out of some hidden chamber of the defunct Inquisition, where it had been subjected to torture. "Who can it be?"--I thought.

At this moment I heard again proceeding from afar the same voice--my voice... "the reason or reasons why" ... it said; as though these words were the unbroken continuation of the same sentence of which it had just repeated the two words "to learn." It sounded near, and yet as from some incalculable distance; giving me then the idea that the long subterranean journey, the subsequent mental reflexions and discoveries, had occupied no time; had been performed during the short, almost instantaneous interval between the first and the middle words of the sentence, begun, at any rate, if not actually pronounced by myself in my room at Kioto, and which it was now finishing, in interrupted, broken phrases, like a faithful echo of my own words and voice...

Forthwith, the hideous, mangled remains began assuming a form, and, to me, but too familiar appearance. The broken parts joined together one to the other, the bones became covered once more with flesh, and I recognized in these disfigured remains--with some surprise, but not a trace of feeling at the sight--my sister's dead husband, my own brother-in-law, whom I had for her sake loved so truly. "How was it, and how did he come to die such a terrible death?"--I asked myself. To put oneself a query seemed, in the state in which I was, to instantly solve it. Hardly had I asked myself the question, when as if in a panorama, I saw the retrospective picture of poor Karl's death, in all its horrid vividness, and with every thrilling detail, every one of which, however, left me then entirely and brutally indifferent. Here he is, the dear old fellow, full of life and joy at the prospect of more lucrative employment from his principal, examining and trying in a wood-sawing factory a monster steam engine just arrived from America. He bends over, to examine more closely an inner arrangement, to tighten a screw. His clothes are caught by the teeth of the revolving wheel in full motion, and suddenly he is dragged down, doubled up, and his limbs half severed, torn off, before the workmen, unacquainted with the mechanism, can stop it. He is taken out, or what remains of him, dead, mangled, a thing of horror, an unrecognisable mass of palpitating flesh and blood! I follow the remains, wheeled as an unrecognizable heap to the hospital, hear the brutally given order that the messengers of death should stop on their way at the house of the widow and orphans. I follow them, and find the unconscious family quietly assembled together. I see my sister, the dear and beloved, and remain indifferent at the sight, only feeling highly interested in the coming scene. My heart, my feelings, even my personality, seem to have disappeared, to have been left behind, to belong to somebody else.

There "I" stand, and witness her unprepared reception of the ghastly news. I realize clearly, without one moment's hesitation or mistake, the effect of the shock upon her, I perceive clearly, following and recording, to the minutest detail, her sensations and the inner process that takes place in her. I watch and remember, missing not one single point. As the corpse is brought into the house for identification

I hear the long agonizing cry, my own name pronounced, and the dull thud of the living body falling upon the remains of the dead one. I followed with curiosity the sudden thrill and the instantaneous perturbation in her brain that follow it, and watch with attention the worm-like, precipitate, and immensely intensified motion of the tubular fibres, the instantaneous change of colour in the cephalic extremity of the nervous system, the fibrous nervous matter passing from white to bright red and then to a dark red, bluish hue. I notice the sudden flash of a phosphorous-like, brilliant Radiance, its tremor and its sudden extinction followed by darkness--complete darkness in the region of memory--as the Radiance, comparable in its form only to a human shape, oozes out suddenly from the top of the head, expands, loses its form and scatters. And I say to myself: "This is insanity; life-long, incurable insanity, for the principle of intelligence is not paralyzed or extinguished temporarily, but has just deserted the tabernacle for ever, ejected from it by the terrible force of the sudden blow ... The link between the animal and the divine essence is broken" ... And as the unfamiliar term "divine" is mentally uttered my "THOUGHT"--laughs.

Suddenly I hear again my far-off yet near voice pronouncing emphatically and close by me the words... "why my sister has so suddenly ceased writing"... And before the two final words "to me" have completed the sentence, I see a long series of sad events, immediately following the catastrophe. I behold the mother, now a helpless, grovelling idiot, in the lunatic asylum attached to the city hospital, the seven younger children admitted into a refuge for paupers. Finally I see the two elder, a boy of fifteen and a girl a year younger, my favourites, both taken by strangers into their service. A captain of a sailing vessel carries away my nephew, an old

Jewess adopts the tender girl. I see the events with all their horrors and thrilling details, and record each, to the smallest detail, with the utmost coolness.

For, mark well: when I use such expressions as horrors etc., they are to be understood as an afterthought. During the whole time of the events described I experienced no sensation of either pain or pity. My feelings seemed to be paralyzed as well as my external senses; it was only after "coming back" that I realized my irretrievable losses to their full extent.

Much of that which I had so vehemently denied in those days, owing to sad personal experience I have to admit now. Had I been told by any one at that time, that man could act and think and feel, irrespective of his brain and senses; nay, that by some mysterious, and to this day, for me, incomprehensible power, he could be transported mentally, thousands of miles away from his body, there to witness not only present but also past events, and remember these by storing them in his memory--I would have proclaimed that man as a madman. Alas, I can do so no longer, for I have become myself that "madman." Ten, twenty, forty, a hundred times during the course of this wretched life of mine, have I experienced and lived over such moments of existence, outside of my body. Accursed be that hour when this terrible power was first awakened in me! I have not even the consolation left of attributing such glimpses of events at a distance to insanity. Madmen rave and see that which exists not in the realm they belong to. My visions have proved invariably correct. But to my narrative of woe.

I had hardly had time to see my unfortunate young niece in her new Israelitish home, when I felt a shock of the same nature as the one that had sent me "swimming" through the bowels of the earth, as I had thought. I opened my eyes in my own room, and the first thing I fixed upon, by accident, was the clock. The hands of the dial showed seven minutes and a half past five!... I had thus passed through these most terrible experiences which it takes me hours to narrate, in precisely half a minute of time!

But this, too, was an afterthought. For one brief instant I recollected nothing of what I had seen. The interval between the time I had glanced at the clock when taking the mirror from the Yamabooshi's hand and this second glance, seemed to me merged in one. I was just opening my lips to hurry on the Yamabooshi with his experiment, when the full remembrance of what I had just seen flashed lightning--like into my brain. Uttering a cry of horror and despair, I felt as though the whole creation were crushing me under its weight. For one moment I remained speechless, the picture of human ruin amid a world of death and desolation. My heart sank down in anguish: my doom was closed; and a hopeless gloom seemed to settle over the rest of my life for ever.

V--RETURN OF DOUBTS

Then came a reaction as sudden as my grief itself. A doubt arose in my mind, which forthwith grew into a fierce desire of denying the truth of what I had seen. A stubborn resolution of treating the whole thing as an empty, meaningless dream, the effect of my overstrained mind, took possession of me. Yes; it was but a lying vision, an idiotic cheating of my own senses, suggesting pictures of death and misery which had been evoked by weeks of incertitude and mental depression. "How could I see all that I have seen in less than half a minute?"--I exclaimed. "The theory of dreams, the rapidity with which the material changes on which our ideas in vision depend, are excited in the hemispherical ganglia, is sufficient to account for the long series of events I have seemed to experience. In dream alone can the relations of space and time be so completely annihilated. The Yamabooshi is for nothing in this disagreeable nightmare. He is only reaping that which has been sown by myself, and, by using some infernal drug, of which his tribe have the secret, he has contrived to make me lose consciousness for a few seconds and see that vision--as lying as it is horrid. Avaunt all such thoughts, I believe them not. In a few days there will be a steamer sailing for Europe ... I shall leave to-morrow!"

This disjointed monologue was pronounced by me aloud, regardless of the presence of my respected friend the Bonze, Tamoora, and the Yamabooshi. The latter was standing before me in the same position as when he placed the mirror in my hands, and kept looking at me calmly, I should perhaps say looking through me, and in dignified silence. The Bonze, whose kind countenance was beaming with sympathy, approached me as he would a sick child, and gently laying his hand on mine, and with tears in his eyes, said: "Friend, you must not leave this city before you have been completely purified of your contact with the lower Daij-Dzins (spirits), who had to be used to guide your inexperienced soul to the places it craved to see. The entrance to your Inner Self must be closed against their dangerous intrusion. Lose no time, therefore, my Son, and allow the holy Master, yonder, to purify you at once."

But nothing can be more deaf than anger once aroused. "The sap of reason" could no longer "quench the fire of passion," and at that moment I was not fit to listen to his friendly voice. His is a face I can never recall to my memory without genuine feeling; his, a name I will ever pronounce with a sigh of emotion; but at that ever memorable hour when my passions were inflamed to white heat, I felt almost a hatred for the kind, good old man, I could not forgive him his interference in the present event. Hence, for all answer, therefore, he received from me a stern rebuke, a violent protest on my part against the idea that I could ever regard the vision I had had, in any other light save that of an empty dream, and his Yamabooshi as anything better than an imposter. "I will leave to-morrow, had I to forfeit my whole fortune as a penalty"--I exclaimed, pale with rage and despair.

"You will repent it the whole of your life, if you do so before the holy man has shut every entrance in you against intruders ever on the watch and ready to enter the open door," was the answer. "The Daij-Dzins will have the best of you."

I interrupted him with a brutal laugh, and a still more brutally phrased enquiry about the fees I was expected to give the

Yamabooshi, for his experiment with me.

"He needs no reward," was the reply. "The order he belongs to is the richest in the world, since its adherents need nothing, for they are above all terrestrial and venal desires. Insult him not, the good man who came to help you out of pure sympathy for your suffering, and to relieve you of mental agony."

But I would listen to no words of reason and wisdom. The spirit of rebellion and pride had taken possession of me, and made me disregard every feeling of personal friendship, or even of simple propriety. Luckily for me, on turning round to order the medican monk out of my presence, I found he had gone.

I had not seen him move, and attributed his stealthy departure to fear at having been detected and understood.

Fool! blind, conceited idiot that I was! Why did I fail to recognize the Yamabooshi's power, and that the peace of my whole life was departing with him, from that moment for ever? But I did so fail. Even the fell demon of my long fears--uncertainty--was now entirely overpowered by that fiend scepticism--the silliest of all. A dull, morbid unbelief, a stubborn denial of the evidence of my own senses, and a determined will to regard the whole vision as a fancy of my overwrought mind, had taken firm hold of me.

"My mind," I argued, "what is it? Shall I believe with the superstitious and the weak that this production of phosphorus and grey matter is indeed the superior part of me; that it can act and see independently of my physical senses? Never! As well believe in the planetary 'intelligences' of the astrologer, as in the 'Daij-Dzins' of my credulous though well-meaning friend, the priest. As well confess one's belief in Jupiter and Sol, Saturn and Mercury, and that these worthies guide their spheres and concern themselves with mortals, as to give one serious thought to the airy nonentities supposed to have guided my 'soul' in its unpleasant dream! I loathe and laugh at the absurd idea. I regard it as a personal insult to the intellect and rational reasoning powers of a man, to speak of invisible creatures, 'subjective intelligences,' and all that kind of insane superstition." In short, I begged my friend the Bonze to spare me his protests, and thus the unpleasantness of breaking with him for ever.

Thus I raved and argued before the venerable Japanese gentleman, doing all in my power to leave on his mind the indelible conviction of my having gone suddenly mad. But his admirable forbearance proved more than equal to my idiotic passion; and he implored me once more, for the sake of my whole future, to submit to certain "necessary purificatory rites."

"Never! Far rather dwell in air, rarified to nothing by the air-pump or wholesome unbelief, than in the dim fog of silly superstition," I argued, paraphrazing Richter's remark. "I will not believe," I repeated; "but as I can no longer bear such uncertainty about my sister and her family, I will return by the first steamer to Europe."

This final determination upset my old acquaintance altogether. His earnest prayer not to depart before I had seen the Yamabooshi once more, received no attention from me.

"Friend of a foreign land!"--he cried, "I pray that you may not repent of your unbelief and rashness. May the 'Holy One' [Kwan-On, the Goddess of Mercy] protect you from the Dzins! For, since you refuse to submit to the process of purification at the hands of the holy Yamabooshi, he is powerless to defend you from the evil influences evoked by your unbelief and defiance of truth. But let me, at this parting hour, I beseach you, let me, an older man who wishes you well, warn you once more and persuade you of things you are still ignorant of. May I speak?"

"Go on and have your say," was the ungracious assent. "But let me warn you, in my turn, that nothing you can say can make of me a believer in your disgraceful superstitions." This was added with a cruel feeling of pleasure in bestowing one more needless insult.

But the excellent man disregarded this new sneer as he had all others. Never shall I forget the solemn earnestness of his parting words, the pitying, remorseful look on his face when he found that it was, indeed, all to no purpose, that by his kindly meant interference he had only led me to my destruction.

"Lend me your ear, good sir, for the last time," he began, "learn that unless the holy and venerable man; who, to relieve your distress, opened your 'soul vision,' is permitted to complete his work, your future life will, indeed, be little worth living. He has to safeguard you against involuntary repetitions of visions of the same character. Unless you consent to it of your own free will, however, you will have to be left in the power of Forces which will harass and persecute you to the verge of insanity. Know that the development of 'Long Vision' [clairvoyance]--which is accomplished at will only by those for whom the Mother of Mercy, the great Kwan-On, has no secrets--must, in the case of the beginner, be pursued with help of the air Dzins (elemental spirits) whose nature is soulless, and hence wicked. Know also that, while the Arihat, 'the destroyer of the enemy,' who has subjected and made of these creatures his servants, has nothing to fear; he who has no power over them becomes their slave. Nay, laugh not in your great pride and ignorance, but listen further. During the time of the vision and while the inner perceptions are directed toward the events they seek, the Daij-Dzin has the seer--when, like yourself, he is an inexperienced tyro--entirely in its power; and for the time being that seer is no longer himself. He partakes of the nature of his 'guide.' The Dali-Dzin, which directs his inner sight, keeps his soul in durance vile, making of him, while the state lasts, a creature like itself. Bereft of his divine light, man is but a soulless being; hence during the time of such connection, he will feel no human emotions, neither pity nor fear, love nor mercy."

"Hold!" I involuntarily exclaimed, as the words vividly brought back to my recollections the indifference with which I had witnessed my sister's despair and sudden loss of reason in my "hallucination," "Hold!...But no; it is still worse madness in me to heed or find any sense in your ridiculous tale! But if you knew it to be so dangerous why have advised the experiment at all?"--I added mockingly.

"It had to last but a few seconds, and no evil could have resulted from it, had you kept your promise to submit to purification," was the sad and humble reply. "I wished you well, my friend, and my heart was nigh breaking to see you suffering day by day. The experiment is harmless enough when directed by one who knows, and becomes dangerous only when the final precaution is neglected. It is the 'Master of Visions,' he who has opened an entrance into your soul, who has to close it by using the Seal of Purification against any further and deliberate ingress of..."

"The 'Master of Visions' forsooth!" I cried, brutally interrupting him, "say rather the Master of Imposture!"

The look of sorrow on his kind old face was so intense and painful to behold that I perceived I had gone too far; but it was too late.

"Farewell, then!" said the old Bonze, rising; and after performing the usual ceremonials of politeness, Tamoora left the house in dignified silence.

VI--I DEPART--BUT NOT ALONE

Several days later I sailed, but during my stay I saw my venerable friend, the Bonze, no more. Evidently on that last, and to me for ever memorable evening, he had been seriously offended with my more than irreverent, my downright insulting remark about one whom he so justly respected. I felt sorry for him, but the wheel of passion and pride was too incessantly at work to permit me to feel a single moment of remorse. What was it that made me so relish the pleasure of wrath, that when, for one instant, I happened to lose sight of my supposed grievance toward the Yamabooshi, I forthwith lashed myself back into a kind of artificial fury against him. He had only accomplished what he had been expected to do, and what he had tacitly promised; not only so, but it was I myself who had deprived him of the possibility of doing more, even for my own protection if I might believe the Bonze--a man whom I knew to be thoroughly honourable and reliable. Was it regret at having been forced by my pride to refuse the proffered precaution, or was it the fear of remorse that made me rake together, in my heart, during those evil hours, the smallest details of the supposed insult to that same suicidal pride? Remorse, as an old poet has aptly remarked, "is like the heart in which it grows: ...
"...if proud and gloomy.
It is a poison-tree, that pierced to the utmost.
Weeps only tears of blood"...

Perchance, it was the indefinite fear of something of that sort which caused me to remain so obdurate, and led me to excuse, under the plea of terrible provocation, even the unprovoked insults that I had heaped upon the head of my kind and all-forgiving friend, the priest. However, it was now too late in the day to recall the words of offence I had uttered; and all I could do was to promise myself the satisfaction of writing him a friendly letter, as soon as I reached home. Fool, blind fool, elated with insolent self-conceit, that I was! So sure did I feel, that my vision was due merely to some trick of the Yamabooshi, that I actually gloated over my coming triumph in writing to the Bonze that I had been right in answering his sad words of parting with an incredulous smile, as my sister and family were all in good health--happy!

I had not been at sea for a week, before I had cause to remember his words of warning!

From the day of my experience with the magic mirror, I perceived a great change in my whole state, and I attributed it, at first, to the mental depression I had struggled against for so many months. During the day I very often found myself absent from the surroundings scenes, losing sight for several minutes of things and persons. My nights were disturbed, my dreams oppressive, and at times horrible. Good sailor I certainly was; and besides, the weather was unusually fine, the ocean as smooth as a pond. Notwithstanding this, I often felt a strange giddiness, and the familiar faces of my fellow-passengers assumed at such times the most grotesque appearances. Thus, a young German I used to know well was once suddenly transformed before my eyes into his old father, whom we had laid in the little burial place of the European colony some three years before. We were talking on deck of the defunct and of a certain business arrangement of his, when Max Grunner's head appeared to me as though it were covered with a strange film. A thick greyish mist surrounded him, and gradually condensing around and upon his healthy countenance, settled suddenly into the grim old head I had myself seen covered with six feet of soil. On another occasion, as the captain was talking of a Malay thief whom he had helped to secure and lodge in goal, I saw near him the yellow, villainous face of a man answering to his description. I kept silence about such hallucinations; but as they became more and more frequent, I felt very much disturbed, though still attributing them to natural causes, such as I had read about in medical books.

One night I was abruptly awakened by a long and loud cry of distress. It was a woman's voice, plaintive like that of a child, full of terror and of helpless despair. I awoke with a start to find myself on land, in a strange room. A young girl, almost a child, was desperately struggling against a powerful middle-aged man, who had surprised her in her own room, and during her sleep. Behind the closed and locked door, I saw listening an old woman, whose face, notwithstanding the fiendish expression upon it, seemed familiar to me, and I immediately recognized it: it was the face of the Jewess who had adopted my niece in the dream I had at Kioto. She had received gold to pay for her share in the foul crime, and was now keeping her part of the covenant ... But who was the victim? O horror unutterable! Unspeakable horror! When I realized the situation after coming back to my normal state, I found it was my own child-niece.

But, as in my first vision, I felt in me nothing of the nature of that despair born of affection that fills one's heart, at the sight of a wrong done to, or a misfortune befalling, those one loves; nothing but a manly indignation in the presence of suffering inflicted upon the weak and the helpless.

I rushed, of course, to her rescue, and seized the wanton, brutal beast by the neck. I fastened upon him with powerful grasp, but, the man heeded it not, he seemed not even to feel my hand. The coward, seeing himself resisted by the girl, lifted his powerful arm and the thick fist, coming down like a heavy hammer upon the sunny locks, felled the child to the ground. It was with a loud cry of the indignation of a stranger, not with that of a tigress defending her cub, that I sprang upon the lewd beast and sought to throttle him. I then remarked, for the first time, that, a shadow myself, I was grasping but another shadow! ...

My loud shrieks and imprecations had awakened the whole steamer. They were attributed to a nightmare. I did not seek to take anyone into my confidence; but, from that day forward, my life became a long series of mental tortures, I could hardly shut my eyes without becoming witness of some horrible deed, some scene of misery, death or crime, whether past, present or even future--as I ascertained later on. It was as though some mocking fiend had taken upon himself the task of making me go through the vision of everything that was bestial, malignant and hopeless, in this world of misery. No radiant vision of beauty or virtue ever lit with the faintest ray these pictures of awe and wretchedness that I seemed doomed to witness. Scenes of wickedness, of murder, of treachery and of lust fell dismally upon my sight, and I was brought face to face with the vilest results of man's passions, the most terrible outcome of his material earthly cravings.

Had the Bonze foreseen, indeed, the dreary results, when he spoke of Daij-Dzins to whom I left "an ingress" "a door open" in me? Nonsense! There must be some physiological, abnormal change in me. Once at Nuremberg, when I have ascertained how false was the direction taken by my fears--I dared not hope for no misfortune at all--these meaningless visions will disappear as they came. The very fact that my fancy follows but one direction, that of pictures of misery, of human passions in their worst, material shape, is a proof, to me, of their unreality.

"If, as you say, man consists of one substance, matter, the object of the physical senses; and if perception with its modes is only the result of the organization of the brain, then should we be naturally attracted but to the material, the earthly"...I thought I heard the familiar voice of the Bonze interrupting my reflections, and repeating an often used argument of his in his discussions with me.

"There are two planes of visions before men," I again heard him say, "the plane of undying love and spiritual aspirations, the efflux from the eternal light; and the plane of restless, ever changing matter, the light in which the misguided Daij-Dzins bathe."

VII--ETERNITY IN A SHORT DREAM

In those days I could hardly bring myself to realize, even for a moment, the absurdity of a belief in any kind of spirits, whether good or bad. I now understood, if I did not believe, what was meant by the term, though I still persisted in hoping that it would finally prove some physical derangement or nervous hallucination. To fortify my unbelief the more, I tried to bring back to my memory all the arguments used against faith in such superstitions, that I had ever read or heard. I recalled the biting sarcasms of Voltaire, the calm reasoning of Hume, and I repeated to myself ad nauseam the words of Rousseau, who said that superstition, "the disturber of Society," could never be too strongly attacked. "Why should the sight, the phantasmagoria, rather"--I argued--"of that which we know in a waking sense to be false, come to affect us at all? Why should---"
"Names, whose sense we see not
Fray us with things that be not?"
One day the old captain was narrating to us the various superstitions to which sailors were addicted; a pompous English missionary remarked that Fielding had declared long ago that "superstition renders a man a fool,"--after which he hesitated for an instant, and abruptly stopped. I had not taken any part in the general conversation; but no sooner had the reverend speaker relieved himself of the quotation than I saw in that halo of vibrating light, which I now noticed almost constantly over every human head on

the steamer, the words of Fielding's next proposition--"and scepticism makes him mad."

I had heard and read of the claims of those who pretend to seership, that they often see the thoughts of people traced in the aura of those present. Whatever "aura" may mean with others, I had now a personal experience of the truth of the claim, and felt sufficiently disgusted with the discovery! I--a clairvoyant! a new horror added to my life, an absurd and ridiculous gift developed, which I shall have to conceal from all, feeling ashamed of it as if it were a case of leprosy. At this moment my hatred to the Yamabooshi, and even to my venerable old friend, the Bonze, knew no bounds. The former had evidently by his manipulations over me while I was lying unconscious, touched some unknown physiological spring in my brain, and by loosing it had called forth a faculty generally hidden in the human constitution; and it was the Japanese priest who had introduced the wretch into my house!

But my anger and my curses were alike useless, and could be of no avail. Moreover, we were already in European waters, and in a few more days we should be at Hamburg. Then would my doubts and fears be set at rest, and I should find, to my intense relief, that although clairvoyance, as regards the reading of human thoughts on the spot, may have some truth in it, the discernment of such events at a distance, as I had dreamed of, was an impossibility for human faculties. Notwithstanding all my reasoning, however, my heart was sick with fear, and full of the blackest presentiments; I felt that my doom was closing. I suffered terribly, my nervous and mental prostration becoming intensified day by day.

The night before we entered port I had a dream.

I fancied I was dead. My body lay cold and stiff in its last sleep, whilst its dying consciousness, which still regarded itself as "I," realizing the event, was preparing to meet in a few seconds its own extinction. It had been always my belief that as the brain preserved heat longer than any of the other organs, and was the last to cease its activity, the thought in it survived bodily death by several minutes. Therefore, I was not in the least surprised to find in my dream that while the frame had already crossed that awful gulf "no mortal e'er repassed," its consciousness was still in the gray twilight, the first shadows of the great Mystery. Thus my THOUGHT wrapped, as I believed, in the remnants, of its now fast retiring vitality, was watching with intense and eager curiosity the approaches of its own dissolution, i.e., of its annihilation. "I" was hastening to record my last impressions, lest the dark mantle of eternal oblivion should envelope me, before I had time to feel and enjoy, the great, the supreme triumph of learning that my life-long convictions were true, that death is a complete and absolute cessation of conscious being. Everything around me was getting darker with every moment. Huge grey shadows were moving before my vision, slowly at first, then with accelerated motion, until they commenced whirling around with an almost vertiginous rapidity. Then, as though that motion had taken place for the purposes of brewing darkness, the object once reached, it slackened its speed, and the darkness became gradually transformed into intense blackness, it ceased altogether. There was nothing now within my immediate perceptions, but that fathomless black Space, as dark as pitch; to me it appeared as limitless and as silent as the shoreless Ocean of Eternity upon which Time, the progeny of man's brain, is for ever gliding, but which it can never cross.

Dream is defined by Cato as "but the image of our hopes and fears." Having never feared death when awake, I felt, in this dream of mine, calm and serene at the idea of my speedy end. In truth, I felt rather relieved at the thought--probably owing to my recent mental suffering--that the end of all, of doubt, of fear for those I loved, of suffering, and of every anxiety, was close at hand. The constant anguish that had been gnawing ceaselessly at my heavy, aching heart for many a long and weary month, had now become unbearable; and if as Seneca thinks, death is but "the ceasing to be what we were before," it was better that I should die. The body is dead; "I," its consciousness--that which is all that remains of me now, for a few moments longer--am preparing to follow. Mental perceptions will get weaker, more dim and hazy with every second of time, until the longed for oblivion envelopes me completely in its cold shroud. Sweet is the magic hand of Death, the great World-Comforter; profound and dreamless is sleep in its unyielding arms. Yea, verily, it is a welcome guest... A calm and peaceful haven amidst the roaring billows of the Ocean of life, whose breakers lash in vain the rock-bound shores of Death. Happy the lonely bark that drifts into the still waters of its black gulf, after having been so long, so cruelly tossed about by the angry waves of sentient life. Moored in it for evermore, needing no longer either sail or rudder, my bark will now find rest. Welcome then, O Death, at this tempting price; and fare thee well, poor body, which, having neither sought it nor derived pleasure from it, I now readily give up!

While uttering this death-chant to the prostrate form before me, I bent over, and examined it with curiosity. I felt the surrounding darkness oppressing me, weighing on me almost tangibly, and I fancied I found in it the approach of the Liberator I was welcoming. And yet how very strange! If real, final Death takes place in our consciousness; if after the bodily death, "I" and my conscious perceptions are one--how is it that these perceptions do not become weaker, why does my brain--action seem as vigorous as ever now ... that I am de facto dead? ... Nor does the usual feeling of anxiety, the "heavy heart" so-called, decrease in intensity; nay, it even seems to become worse ... unspeakably so! ... How long it takes for full oblivion to arrive!...Ah, here's my body again!...Vanished out of sight for a second or two, it reappears before me once more ... How white and ghastly it looks! Yet ... its brain cannot be quite dead, since "I," its consciousness, am still acting, since we two fancy that we still are, that we live and think, disconnected from our creator and its ideating cells.

Suddenly I felt a strong desire to see how much longer the progress of dissolution was likely to last, before it placed its last seal on the brain and rendered it inactive. I examined my brain in its cranial cavity, through the (to me) entirely transparent walls and roof of the skull, and even touched the brain-matter ... How or with whose hands, I am now unable to say; but the impression of the slimy, intensely cold matter produced a very strong impression on me, in that dream. To my great dismay, I found that the blood having entirely congealed and the brain-tissues having themselves undergone a change that would no longer permit any molecular action, it became impossible for me to account for the phenomena now taking place with myself. Here was I,--or my consciousness which is all one--standing apparently entirely disconnected from my brain which could no longer function ... But I had no time left for reflection. A new and most extraordinary change in my perceptions had taken place and now engrossed my whole attention ... What does this signify? ...

The same darkness was around me as before, a black, impenetrable space, extending in every direction. Only now, right before me, in whatever direction I was looking, moving with me which way soever I moved, there was a gigantic round clock; a disc, whose large white face shone ominously on the ebony-black background. As I looked at its huge dial, and at the pendulum moving to and fro regularly and slowly in Space, as if its swinging meant to divide eternity, I saw its needles pointing to seven minutes past five. "The hour at which my torture had commenced at Kioto!" I had barely found time to think of the coincidence, when to my unutterable horror, I felt myself going through the same, the identical, process that I had been made to experience on that memorable and fatal day. I swam underground, dashing swiftly through the earth; I found myself once more in the pauper's grave and recognized my brother-in-law in the mangled remains; I witnessed his terrible death; entered my sister's house; followed her agony, and saw her go mad. I went over the same scenes without missing a single detail of them. But, alas! I was no longer iron-bound in the calm indifference that had then been mine, and which in that first vision had left me as unfeeling to my great misfortune as if I had been a heartless thing of rock. My mental tortures were now becoming beyond description and well-nigh unbearable. Even the settled despair, the never-ceasing anxiety I was constantly experiencing when awake, had become now, in my dream and in the face of this repetition of vision and events, as an hour of darkened sunlight compared to a deadly cyclone. Oh! how I suffered in this wealth and pomp of infernal horrors, to which the conviction of the survival of man's consciousness after death--for in that dream I firmly believed that my body was dead--added the most terrifying of all!

The relative relief I felt, when, after going over the last scene, I saw once more the great white face of the dial before me was not of long duration. The long, arrow-shaped needle was pointing on the colossal disk at--seven minutes and a half-past five o'clock. But, before I had time to well realize the change, the needle moved slowly backwards, stopped at precisely the seventh minute, and--O cursed fate! ... I found myself driven into a repetition of the same series over again! Once more I swam underground, and saw, and heard, and suffered every torture that hell can provide; I passed through every mental anguish known to man or fiend. I returned to see the fatal dial and its needle--after what appeared to me an eternity--moved, as before, only half a minute forward. I beheld it, with renewed terror, moving back again, and felt myself propelled forward anew. And so it went on, and on, and on, time after time, in what seemed to me an endless succession, a series which never had any beginning, nor would it ever have an end ...

Worst of all; my consciousness, my "I," had apparently acquired the phenomenal capacity of trebling, quadruping, and even of decuplating itself. I lived, felt and suffered, in the same space of time, in half-a-dozen different places at once, passing over various events of my life, at different epochs and under the most dissimilar circumstances; though predominant over all was my spiritual experience at Kioto. Thus as in the famous fugue in Don Giovanni, the heart-rending notes of Elvira's aria of despair ring high above, but interfere in no way with the melody of the minuet, the song of seduction, and the chorus, so I went over and over my travailed woes, the feelings of agony unspeakable at the awful sights of my vision, the repetition of which blunted in no wise even a single pang of my despair and horror; nor did these feelings weaken in the least scenes and events entirely disconnected with the first one, that I was living through again, or interfere in any way the one with the other. It was a maddening experience! A series of contrapuntal, mental phantasmagoria from real life. Here was I, during the same half-a-minute of time, examining with cold curiosity the mangled remains of my sister's husband; following with the same indifference the effects of the news on her brain, as in my first Kioto vision, and feeling at the same time hell-torture for these very events, as when I returned to consciousness. I was listening to the philosophical discourses of the Bonze, every word of which I heard and understood, and was trying to laugh him to scorn. I was again a child, then a youth, hearing my mother's and my sweet sister's voices, admonishing me and teaching duty to all men. I was saving a friend from drowning, and was sneering at his aged father who thanks me for saving a "soul" yet unprepared to meet his Maker.

"Speak of dual consciousness, you psycho-physiologists!"--I cried, in one of the moments when agony, mental and as it seemed to me physical also, had arrived at a degree of intensity which would have killed a dozen living men; "speak of your psychological and physiological experiments, you schoolmen, puffed up with pride and book-learning! Here am I to give you the lie..." And now I was reading the works and holding converse with learned professors and lecturers, who had led me to my fatal scepticism. And, while arguing the impossibility of consciousness divorced from its brain, I was shedding tears of blood over the supposed fate of my nieces and nephews. More terrible than all: I knew, as only a liberated consciousness can know, that all I had seen in my vision at Japan, and all that I was seeing and hearing over and over again now, was true in every point and detail, that it was a long string of ghastly and terrible, still of real, actual, facts.

For, perhaps, the hundredth time, I had rivetted my attention on the needle of the clock, I had lost the number of my gyrations and was fast coming to the conclusion that they would never stop, that consciousness is, after all, indestructible, and that this was to be my punishment in Eternity. I was beginning to realize from personal experience how the condemned sinners would feel--"were not eternal damnation a logical and mathematical impossibility in an ever-progressing Universe"--I still found the force to argue. Yea indeed; at this hour of my ever-increasing agony, my consciousness--now my synonym for "I"--had still the power of revolting at certain theological claims, of denying all their propositions, all--save ITSELF ... No; I denied the independent nature of my consciousness no longer, for I knew it now to be such. But is it eternal withal? O thou incomprehensible and terrible Reality! But if thou art eternal, who then art thou?--since there is no diety, no God. Whence dost thou come, and when didst thou first appear, if thou art not a part of the cold body lying yonder? And whither dost thou lead me, who am thyself, and shall our thought and fancy have an end? What is thy real name, thou unfathomable REALITY, and impenetrable MYSTERY! Oh, I would fain annihilate thee ... "Soul--Vision"!--who speaks of Soul, and whose voice is this? ... It says that I see now for myself, that there is a Soul in man, after all... I deny this. My Soul, my vital Soul, or the Spirit of life, has expired with my body, with the gray matter of my brain, This "I" of mine, this consciousness, is not yet proven to me as eternal. Reincarnation, in which the Bonze felt so anxious I should believe, may be true ... Why not? Is not the flower born year after year from the same root? Hence this "I" once separated from, its brain, losing its balance and calling forth such a host of visions ... before reincarnating.

I was again face to face with the inexorable, fatal clock. And as I was watching its needle, I heard the voice of the Bonze, coming out of the depths of its white face, saying: "In this case, I fear you would have only to open and to shut the temple door, over and over again, during a period which, however short, would seem to you an eternity..."

The clock had vanished, darkness made room for light, the voice of my old friend was drowned by a multitude of voices overhead on deck; and I awoke in my berth, covered with a cold perspiration, and faint with terror.

VIII--A TALE OF WOE

We were at Hamburg, and no sooner had I seen my partners, who could hardly recognise me, than with their consent and good wishes I started for Nuremberg.
Half-an-hour after my arrival, the last doubt with regard to the correctness of my vision had disappeared. The reality was worse than any expectations could have made it, and I was henceforward doomed to the most desolate life. I ascertained that I had seen the terrible tragedy, with all its heart-rending details. My brother-in-law, killed under the wheels of a machine; my sister, insane, and now rapidly sinking toward her end; my niece--the sweet flower of nature's fairest work--dishonoured, in a den of infamy; the little children dead of a contagious disease in an orphanage; my last surviving nephew at sea, no one knew where. A whole house, a home of love and peace, scattered; and I, left alone, a witness of this world of death, of desolation and dishonour. The news filled me with infinite despair, and I sank helpless before the wholesale, dire disaster, which rose before me all at once. The shock proved too much, and I fainted. The last thing I heard before entirely losing my consciousness was a remark of the Burgmeister: "Had you, before leaving Kioto, telegraphed to the city authorities of your whereabouts, and of your intention of coming home to take charge of your young relatives, we might have placed them elsewhere, and thus have saved them from their fate. No one knew that the children had a well-to-do relative. They were left paupers

and had to be dealt with as such. They were comparatively strangers in Nuremberg, and under the unfortunate circumstances you could have hardly expected anything else ... I can only express my sincere sorrow."

It was this terrible knowledge that I might, at any rate, have saved my young niece from her unmerited fate, but that through my neglect I had not done so, that was killing me. Had I but followed the friendly advice of the Bonze, Tamoora, and telegraphed to the authorities some weeks previous to my return much might have been avoided. It was all this, coupled with the fact that I could no longer doubt clairvoyance and clairaudience--the possibility of which I had so long denied--that brought me so heavily down upon my knees. I could avoid the censure of my fellow-creatures but I could never escape the stings of my conscience, the reproaches of my own aching heart--no, not as long as I lived! I cursed my stubborn scepticism, my denial of facts, my early education, I cursed myself and the whole world... .

For several days I contrived not to sink beneath my load, for I had a duty to perform to, the dead and to the living. But my sister once rescued from the pauper's asylum, placed under the care of the best physicians, with her daughter to attend to her last moments, and the Jewess, whom I had brought to confess her crime, safely lodged in goal--my fortitude and strength suddenly abandoned me. Hardly a week after my arrival I was myself no better than a raving maniac, helpless in the strong grip of a brain fever. For several weeks I lay between life and death, the terrible disease defying the skill of the best physicians. At last my strong constitution prevailed, and--to my lifelong sorrow--they proclaimed me saved.

I heard the news with a bleeding heart. Doomed to drag the loathsome burden of life henceforth alone, and in constant

remorse; hoping for no help or remedy on earth, and still refusing to believe in the possibility of anything better than a short survival of consciousness beyond the grave, this unexpected return to life added only one more drop of gall to my bitter feelings. They were hardly soothed by the immediate return, during the first days of my convalescence, of those unwelcome and unsought for visions, whose correctness and reality I could deny no more. Alas the day! they were no longer in my sceptical, blind mind.
"The children of an idle brain,
Begot of nothing but vain Fantasy";
but always the faithful photographs of the real woes and sufferings of my fellow creatures, of my best friends... Thus I found myself doomed, whenever I was left for a moment alone, to the helpless torture of a chained Prometheus. During the still hours of night, as though held by some pitiless iron hand, I found myself led to my sister's bedside, forced to watch there hour after hour, and see the silent disintegration of her wasted organism; to witness and feel the sufferings that her own tenantless brain could no longer reflect or convey to her perceptions. But there was something still more horrible to barb the dart that could never be extricated. I had to look, by day, at the childish innocent face of my young niece, so sublimely simple and guileless in her pollution; and to witness, by night, how the full knowledge and recollection of her dishonour, of her young life now for ever blasted, came to her in her dreams, as soon as she was asleep. The dreams took an objective form to me, as they had done on the steamer; I had to live them over again, night after night, and feel the same terrible despair. For now, since I believed in the reality of seership, and had come to the conclusion that in our bodies lies hidden, as in the caterpillar, the chrysalis which may contain in its turn

the butterfly--the symbol of the soul--I no longer remained indifferent, as of yore, to what I witnessed in my Soul-life. Something had suddenly developed in me, had broken loose from its icy cocoon. Evidently I no longer saw only in consequence of the identification of my inner nature with a Daij-Dzin; my visions arose in, consequence of a direct personal psychic development, the fiendish creatures only taking care that I should see nothing of an agreeable or elevating nature. Thus, now, not an unconscious pang in my dying sister's emaciated body, not a thrill of horror in my niece's restless sleep at the recollection of the crime perpetrated upon her, an innocent child, but found a responsive echo in my bleeding heart. The deep fountain of sympathetic love and sorrow had gushed out from the physical heart, and was now loudly echoed by the awakened soul separated from the body. Thus had I to drain the cup of misery to the very dregs! Woe is me, it was a daily and nightly torture! Oh, how I mourned over my proud folly; how I was punished for having neglected to avail myself at Moto of the proffered purification, for now I had come to believe even in the efficacy of the latter. The Daij-Dzin had indeed obtained control over me; and the fiend had let loose all the dogs of hell upon his victim... .

At last the awful gulf was reached and crossed. The poor insane martyr dropped into her dark, and now welcome grave, leaving behind her, but for a few short months, her young, her first-born, daughter. Consumption made short work of that tender girlish frame. Hardly a year after my arrival, I was left alone in the whole wide world, my only surviving nephew having expressed a desire to follow his sea-faring career.

And now, the sequel of my sad story is soon told. A wreck, a prematurely old man, looking at thirty as though sixty winters had passed over my doomed head, and owing to the never-ceasing visions, myself daily on the verge of insanity, I suddenly formed a desperate resolution. I would return to Kioto and seek out the Yamabooshi. I would prostrate myself at the feet of the holy man, and would not leave him until he had recalled the Frankenstein he had raised, the Frankenstein with whom at the time, it was I, myself, who would, not part, through my insolent pride and unbelief.

Three months later I was in my Japanese home again, and I at-once sought out my old, venerable Bonze, Tamoora Hideyeri, I now implored him to take me without an hour's delay to the Yamabooshi, the innocent cause of my daily tortures. His answer but placed the last, the supreme seal on my doom and tenfold intensified my despair. The Yamabooshi had left the country for lands unknown! He had departed one fine morning into the interior, on a pilgrimage, and according to custom, would be absent, unless natural death shortened the period, for no less than seven years! ...

In this mischance, I applied for help and protection to other learned Yamabooshis; and though well aware how useless it was in my case to seek efficient cure from any other "adept," my excellent old friend did everything he could to help me in my misfortune. But it was to no purpose, and the canker-worm of my life's despair could not be thoroughly extricated. I found from them that not one of these learned men could promise to relieve me entirely from the demon of clairvoyant obsession. It was he who raised certain Daij-Dzins, calling on them to show futurity, or things that had already come to pass, who alone had full control over them. With kind sympathy, which I had now learned to appreciate, the holy men invited me to join the group of their disciples, and learn from them what I could do for myself. "Will alone, faith in your own soul-powers, can help you now," they said. "But it may take several years to undo even a part of the great mischief," they added. "A Daij-Dzin is easily dislodged in the beginning; if left alone, he takes possession of a man's nature and it becomes almost impossible to uproot the fiend without killing his victim."

Persuaded that there was nothing but this left for me to do, I gratefully assented, doing my best to believe in all that these holy men believed in, and yet ever failing to do so in my heart. The demon of unbelief and all-denial seemed rooted in me more firmly ever than the Daij-Dzin. Still I did all I could do, decided as I was not to lose my last chance of salvation. Therefore, I proceeded without delay to, free myself from the world and my commercial obligations, in order to live for several years an independent life. I settled my accounts with my Hamburg partners and severed my connection with the firm. Notwithstanding considerable financial losses resulting from such a precipitate liquidation, I found myself, after closing the accounts, a far richer man than I had thought I was. But wealth had no longer any attraction for me, now that I had no one to share it with, no one to work for. Life had become a burden; and such was my indifference to my future, that while giving away all my fortune to my nephew--in case he should return alive from his sea voyager--should have neglected entirely even a small provision for myself, had not my native partner interfered and insisted upon my making it. I now recognized, with Lao-tze, that Knowledge was the only firm hold for a man to trust to, as it is the only one that cannot be shaken by any tempest. Wealth is a weak anchor in the days of sorrow, and self-conceit the most fatal counsellor. Hence I followed the advice of my friends, and laid aside for myself a modest sum, which would be sufficient to assure me a small income for life, or if I ever left my new friends and instructors. Having settled my earthly accounts and disposed of my belongings at Kioto, I joined the "Masters of the Long Vision," who took me to their mysterious abode. There I remained for several years, studying very earnestly and in the most complete solitude, seeing no one but a few of the members of our religious community.

Many are the mysteries of nature that I have fathomed since then, and many secret folio from the library of Tzionene have I devoured, obtaining thereby mastery over several kinds of invisible beings of a lower order. But the great secret of power over the terrible Daij-Dzin I could not get. It remains in the possession of a very limited number of the highest Initiates of Lao-tze, the great majority of the Yamabooshis themselves being ignorant how to obtain such mastery over the dangerous Elemental. One who would reach such power of control would have to become entirely identified with the Yamabooshis, to accept their views and beliefs, and to attain the highest degree of Initiation. Very naturally, I was found unfit to join the Fraternity, owing to many insurmountable reasons besides my congenital and ineradicable scepticism, though I tried hard to believe. Thus, partially relieved of my affliction and taught how to conjure the unwelcome visions away, I still remained, and do remain to this day, helpless to prevent their forced appearance before me now and then.

It was after assuring myself of my unfitness for the exalted position of an independent Seer and Adept that I reluctantly gave up any further trial. Nothing had been heard of the holy man, the first innocent cause of my misfortune; and the old Bonze himself, who occasionally visited me in my retreat, either could not, or would not, inform me of the whereabouts of the Yamabooshi. When, therefore, I had to give up all hope of his ever relieving me entirely from my fatal gift, I resolved to return to Europe, to settle in solitude for the rest of my life. With this object in view, I purchased through my late partners the Swiss chalet in which my hapless sister and I were born, where I had grown up under her care, and selected it for my future hermitage.

When bidding me farewell for ever on the steamer which took me back to my fatherland, the good old Bonze tried to console me for my disappointments. "My son," he said, "regard all that happened to you as your Karma--a just retribution. No one who had subjected himself willingly to the power of a Daij-Dzin can ever hope to become a Rahat (an Adept), a high-souled Yamabooshi--unless immediately purified. At best, as in your case, he may become fitted to oppose and to successfully fight off the fiend. Like a scar left after a poisonous wound the race of a Daij-Dzin can never be effaced from the Soul until purified by a new rebirth Withal, feel not dejected, but be of good cheer in your affliction, since it has led you to acquire true knowledge, and to accept many a truth you would have otherwise rejected with contempt. And of this priceless knowledge, acquired through suffering and personal efforts--no Daij-Dzin can ever deprive you. Fare thee well, then, and may the Mother of Mercy, the great Queen of Heaven, afford you comfort and protection."

We parted, and since then I have led the life of an anchorite, in constant solitude and study. Though still occasionally afflicted, I do not regret the years I have passed under the instruction of the Yamabooshis, but feel gratified for the knowledge received. Of the priest Tamoora Hideyeri I think always with sincere affection and respect. I corresponded regularly with him to the day of his death; an event which, with all its to me painful details, I had the unthanked-for privilege of witnessing across the seas, at the very hour in which it occurred.

INTRODUCTION	3
I--THE STRANGER'S STORY	7
III--PSYCHIC MAGIC	24
IV--A VISION OF HORROR	29
V--RETURN OF DOUBTS	35
VI--I DEPART--BUT NOT ALONE	41
VII--ETERNITY IN A SHORT DREAM	46
VIII--A TALE OF WOE	56

Printed in Great Britain
by Amazon